They tell me about the believers ,and how they will help me succeed.

I wonder who they are,
do they have pictures
on the dresser?

and how could they even help
me become a pro wrestler?

Will I meet them when I make
it to the NBA ?

Or maybe I'll see them on my spaceship going into space.

I wonder if they'll like me more when I become a fire fighter?

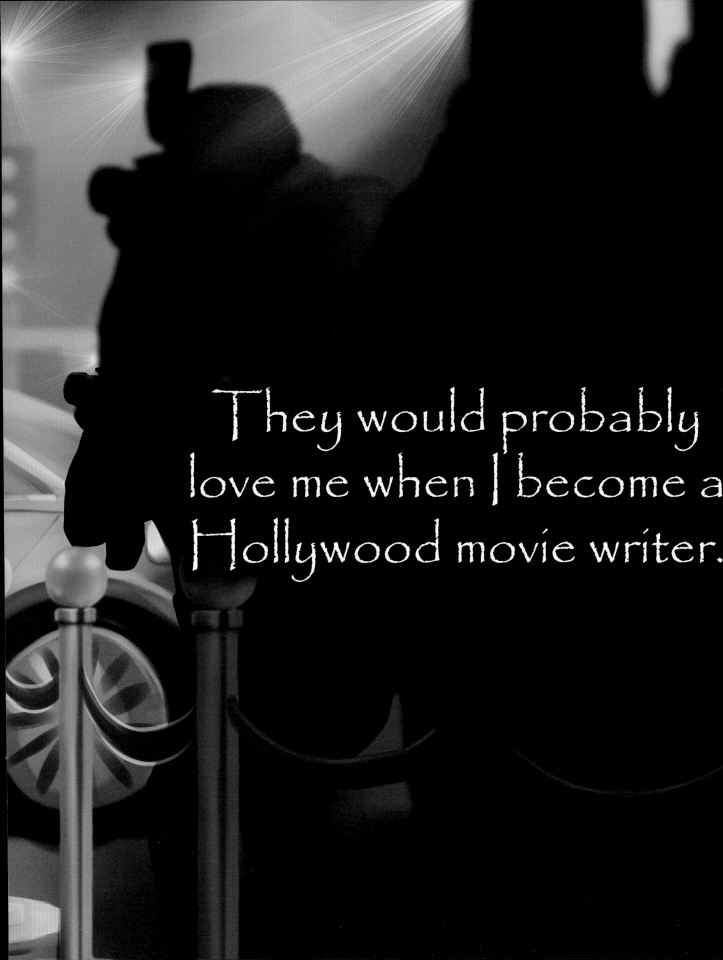

They would probably love me when I become a Hollywood movie writer.

I want to meet the believers,
but where should I start?

And then I remembered,
they're in my heart.

My parents told me they will be there when I chase my dreams.

Friends and family, all there to make sure I succeed.